A Perfect Place

Joshua's Oregon Trail Diary

· Book Two ·

by Patricia Hermes

Scholastic Inc. New York

Willamette Valley, Oregon
1848

October 13, 1848

Early morning and misty.

Last night, in the darkest part of the night, we woke up to a snuffling, huffing sound. An animal was outside our tent. We listened as it circled around and around us. We could tell it was big because the ground moved beneath us. Suddenly, the creature butted against our tent. It was trying to push it over! The tent swayed and rocked around us. My heart started to race. Little Becky cried out. Ma whispered, "Hush." Pa reached out and squeezed my hand, warning me to stay still.

We lay still a long while. Finally, after about forever, the animal shuffled away.

This morning, me and Pa went outside. We saw a paw print in the ground, a bear print. I put my foot inside it. It was two times as big as my shoe, maybe three times. We think it was a grizzly. Pa says he'll sleep with his rifle beside him from now on.

Back in St. Joseph, Missouri, that would have scared me. Now, I don't think I even mind a grizzly bear.

October 14

More rain and mist.

This is my second diary. The first I finished when we got here not quite two weeks ago at the end of the trail. So I guess I should tell a bit about how we got to the Willamette Valley in Oregon. Grampa says it's my job to write in my journal. *Someone has to record such foolishness,* is what he says.

Now, though, Pa is calling me to milk our cow, Laurie. I'll write more later.

Later

This is how we came to be here: Pa, Ma, Grampa, my baby sister, Becky, and me — Joshua Martin McCullough — left our home in St. Joseph, Missouri, last April. We came with lots of other people in wagons across the prairie. My best friend and cousin, Charlie Granger, came, too. He came with his ma and pa, Aunt Lizzie and Uncle Arthur, and his little sister, Rachel. His ma and my ma are twins. One wouldn't come without the other. On the trail though, Charlie's sister, Rachel, had an accident and got killed. In nightmares, I still see her hanging by her twisted gown from the axle of the wagon.

The trail was hard. It rained. Then the

sun beat down on us. It was so hot even my little dog, Buster, got burned feet. Then wind blew sand in our eyes. Flies were everywhere. Hailstorms pelted us. We crossed land as flat as dinner plates. We crossed mountains so high we had to take our wagons apart. Then we had to haul them up by chains and lower them again. And then we put them back together — if we could! (Sometimes we couldn't and we left things behind. That made the women cry.) We crossed about a thousand rivers. We met Indians. Some were scary, but most were kind to us. We met up with wolves. Folks fell off wagons and got themselves killed. I even got lost. I've never been so happy as I was when Grampa came galloping back to find me on that black, black night. And sometimes — well, sometimes things were good. Charlie and I, we got to ride horses and corral the cattle, and help set up and break camp. It was like we were grown up — like men. And you could just see how proud Grampa was of me. Some nights, stars shone down on us, and the men sang and the women danced.

Now at last we're here, at the end of the Oregon Trail. We're in the Willamette Valley. Pa smiles. He's happy because we'll have our own land. Lots and lots of land, Pa says, the whole of God's outdoors! And Ma's happy just to be here at last.

I'm happy, too. But I sure wish Ma would see how grown up I got on the trail. She still acts like I'm hardly more than a baby.

October 15

Rain again. And mist. Everything's wet all the time. We hang things around the tent to dry. But they never do dry. Last night, I woke and the rain had soaked right through the tent.

It was wetting my sleeping roll and dripping down my neck. I'm no sissy, but I sure hate sleeping wet. I crawled out and checked around the tent to see if I could find a dry spot. Ma and Pa were sleeping and if they were wet, it didn't seem to keep them awake none. Little Becky was sleeping, too. With my hand, I tested the tent above her head. It was dry, so I got into the sleeping roll with her.

It made me laugh, because she snuggled right up to me, one skinny arm around my neck. I think she liked having her brother near.

I tell God thank you many times that Becky didn't die like little Rachel.

October 16

Grampa's always telling me *just use your head*. He means I should think about things, make good judgments. Be grown up. I used my head a lot on the trail. And yesterday, I told Ma that I feel grown up now. She said, "Nine years old and you think you're grown up? I'll let you know when you're grown up, young man."

Then she sent me out to get sand to scrub up some pots down in the creek.

Seems like a ma is always wanting to keep you a baby. She's afraid to even let me go explore the woods.

October 17

Grampa has always been my best friend. He lets me do things Ma doesn't let me do, grown up things. Like on the trail, he let me go hunting with him. I even shot and killed a buffalo. He came with us to Oregon because there was nothing in Missouri to hold him back. Grandma died long ago. But on the trail, he found himself a new bride. Her name is Miss Emmaline. But now that they're married, what should I call her? I can't call her Grandma. She's younger than Ma, even. (She's also prettier, but I'd never say that to Ma.)

I'm glad he has Miss Emmaline. She seems to suit him just fine.

October 18

We're camping for now on Abernathy Green. It's owned by a man named George Abernathy. He also owns a big general store in Oregon City. He lets us camp here till our houses are built. Ma says he must be a very kind man. All of us settlers have made a little town here — tents side by side. It's our own neighborhood, just like on the trail. Next to us are Aunt Lizzie and Uncle Arthur and my cousin, Charlie.

The Meaneys are here, too. Mrs. Meaney was real awful on the trail, but seems nicer now. There's the Druckers and their daughter, Bobbi. She's a good friend even though she's a girl. But now her pa has decided to look for gold. They'll be leaving us soon and I'll miss her something bad. There's the Hulls with their ten children. (They had eleven, but one died before we got here.) One of their sons is named Frederick. He has a mouth like a rattlesnake. He just buzzes on and on, rattling away and saying nothing. There's Mrs. Gibbons and her two babies. She had three babies, but one of hers died on the trail, and her husband died, too. Mrs. Hull takes care of all of them. And there's the Wests. They left us for a while, but then came back. I don't think anyone is glad to have them back. Mr. West is the meanest man I've ever met. His wife and his son, Adam, are scared to death of him. And there's lots of other folks, like Miss Emmaline's sister. Pa says it's a lot like any other neighborhood. Most folks are good. Some are not so good.

October 19

The women visit back and forth and there's a lot of talking and laughing. We're all just so glad to be here. But now, everybody's beginning to get restless. We talk about land and who will build near who. The women want the men to start building right now. But it's the rainy season. The men argue that it's no time to build. Also, there's talk of gold in California. Some men want to go there and get rich and then come back in the spring.

That's what the Druckers did. They left this morning and I didn't even get to say good-bye. Miss Emmaline's sister went with them. Miss Emmaline is awful sad to see her go. Pa says those people are fools. Secretly though, I wonder. Maybe we should go, too. But Pa says this is what we came here for — land, homes.

I told Pa that we should start building, anyway. Who cares about a little rain? We walked two thousand miles, and half of it in the rain.

October 20

This morning, Pa, me, Uncle Arthur, and Charlie went looking for a place to build. Pa asked Grampa to come, too, but he said no. We kept stopping and looking. Here? Or there? Each family can choose a whole square mile. Ma and Aunt Lizzie want houses side by side. They want to be high on a hill to watch the sunrise and sunset. Pa and Uncle Arthur say the valley is better because it's more fertile.

We walked in a big circle. After a while, just on the far side of where we've been camping, I found it. Actually, I think maybe my dog, Buster, found it. He chased a rabbit up a wooded hill. When we followed him, we saw how we were high, high up, overlooking the valley. I told Pa it was the perfect spot — a hill for Ma, and a fertile valley for crops.

Pa agreed. He says it's fertile all right. We'll have to clear about a thousand trees.

October 21

Rain and mist. Again.

Tonight, Ma said she hopes to have our house built by Christmas. Pa just smiled and said, "Wait and see."

Sudden like, words burst out of Ma. She said she's sick and tired of waiting. The minute the words were out of her mouth, I could see she felt ashamed. She looked down at her plate and tears came to her eyes. Pa put a hand on her hand. Becky came and laid her head in Ma's lap.

Poor Ma. She hardly ever complains. She rarely even complained on the trail. Lately though, I notice things get her down. Maybe it's the rain.

October 22

Today, the sun was shining for a change. Ma said she'd take advantage of the sun to do her washing. She made me stay in camp to watch Becky. She's always scared Becky will wander off and get lost. I think she's scared I'll get lost, too, though she doesn't say that. Ma and Aunt Lizzie washed quilts and blankets. Charlie and I helped them wring out the water. That's hard work, but I've gotten real strong.

I told Charlie that I'm maybe as strong as Pa now. Charlie said he's stronger than that. We started to arm wrestle to prove who's stronger, and we both almost tumbled into Ma's washing bucket. She shook her head at us. She said we're both getting too big for our britches.

October 23

This morning, Pa and I took Ma and Becky to see the land we've chosen. Aunt Lizzie is going to have a baby soon, so she didn't come. She said she'd trust Ma to decide. When Ma saw the hill and valley, her eyes got big. And then she started to cry. At first, I was scared.

Didn't she like this place? But then I saw they were happy tears. She said it was perfect. Then I heard her say soft-like to Pa, "A perfect place for our new family."

New family? I guess she means Aunt Lizzie's new baby. Or does she?

October 24

Last night, we all sat around the fire. Ma was bubbling like a teakettle, telling Aunt Lizzie about the land. It was so good to hear Ma sounding so happy. And then, after a bit of talking, sudden-like, Ma says, "Why don't we build one big house — not two? It will go faster that way."

And just like that, Aunt Lizzie agreed.

Ma said, "We'll share one big kitchen."

Aunt Lizzie said, "And one main room."

They went on and on. One side of the house would be for us. And Uncle Arthur and Aunt Lizzie and Charlie and the new baby would have the other side.

"What about Grampa?" I said.

Ma squinched up her eyes in that annoyed way she gets. "He's making his own plans," she said.

So that's how it will be. Pa says it's good. It means one roof, one set of walls. Uncle Arthur said if it makes the women happy, he's happy.

I know what he means. Seems men are always happier when the women are happy.

October 25

Ma fusses over Aunt Lizzie so. I think that's another reason Ma wants to share a house — so they can share the baby. Besides Becky and me, Ma had five other babies. They all died soon after they got born. I know Ma thinks that in Oregon, babies might live longer. Who knows? Maybe they will. I hope Aunt Lizzie's baby will live a long, long time, not like little Rachel.

October 26

This morning, Pa and me and Uncle Arthur and Charlie set out for our land with the oxen. First, Pa staked out the land. Then we worked till sundown cutting trees and hauling away the stumps.

It's hard work. It's hard for us, and hard for the oxen. They're still weak from the long trip. But we all did our best. And we still have a whole lot more to do. I don't mind. I'd clear a million trees by myself to get a start on a house for Ma.

October 27

Another day of land clearing for us. But some of the men here aren't doing anything. They hang around the green talking about packing up for California. Most of the women in camp say they won't budge. I heard Mrs. Hull talking to Mr. Hull. She put her face right in his face. "Not one foot farther," she said. "Not even one inch!"

Mr. Hull put up his hands and backed away from her. "Yes, dear," he said. "Yes, my dear."

I don't know about the other families. But I'm pretty sure the Hulls will stay put.

October 28

At supper tonight, Pa and Ma were talking. Ma again said she hoped by Christmas we'd be in our house.

Pa put a hand on her hand. He said, "More likely spring."

I thought Ma's face would fall to her lap. But she just shrugged and sighed.

Six more months in a wet tent? It's raining again tonight. It rained yesterday. It'll probably rain tomorrow. This is what I think: The sun never shines in Oregon.

October 29

I know the secret to getting sunshine. I'll just write: The sun never shines. And just like that — the sun will shine. This morning, the sun crept over the trees, lighting the green and making everything glitter. A breeze moved the trees. Drops of water glistened everywhere. I watched Becky run after my little dog, Buster, who had wandered onto the green. In Missouri, Becky couldn't run or she'd cough. Sometimes she coughed so hard, her lips got blue. But on the trail, she hardly coughed at all — not even with all the dust. She hasn't coughed here, either. This morning, she caught Buster and fell down laughing. The way Buster's tongue was hanging out, I swear he was laughing, too.

I couldn't help myself. I had to go out and wrestle with both of them.

October 30

Two days of sunshine.

Tonight, as the sun was setting, I looked around me. Everything was pink and soft looking. Even our muddy campground looked pink.

Pa was humming softly, just like he used to do. Ma and Aunt Lizzie were chattering while they cooked supper.

Becky was talking to her little doll. I heard

her ask the doll if she was happy. And then, she made up a different voice, like the doll was answering her back. The doll said, "Yes."

Funny how sunshine can make such a difference.

October 31

Three days of sun!

Later

Ma still treats me like a baby! Charlie and I want so bad to go and explore the woods. But Ma won't hear a word of it. She won't let me leave her sight unless I'm with Pa. I know it's because I got lost on the trail that time. But I'm not going to get lost here. Tonight, I told Grampa that Ma acts like I'm no older than Becky.

Grampa just smiled and put his hand on my shoulder. I waited for him to agree. But he didn't say anything.

Later though, I saw him talking quietly to Pa. I wonder what he said.

November 1

A new month.

Grampa must have had a talk with Pa. Because today, Pa set out a kind of boundary where Charlie and I can go. We can go between the two rivers on either side of Abernathy Green. We can go as far as the second hill in front of us. And in back, we can go to the clearing.

Pa said it was real important that we not cross those boundaries. It's too easy for a person to get lost. He says that even an experienced woodsman can get lost. Besides, he says, there are Indians all about. Some are friendly like the Plains Indians. But some are not.

Charlie and I are real excited.

Our pas are giving us a day off from clearing land tomorrow. Now, if only the sun will shine.

Tonight, I went and told Grampa thank you. I knew it was because of him that I can go. He smiled and said what he always says, "Just use your head."

November 2

The sun is shining! As soon as it got light, I milked Laurie, then collected and split the firewood. Then, I sat down to breakfast with Ma and Pa and Becky. Ma frowned at me all through breakfast but she didn't say a word. Pa was silent, too. I think Ma is mad at Pa for letting me go. So I tried extra hard to be polite, and not gobble my food. But I could hardly wait to get away.

Night

As soon as Charlie and I got away from the green and into the woods, we found a trail. At first, we thought it an Indian trail. We followed it, walking quiet like Indians do. We followed it right down to the edge of a pond. And there we realized that it was no Indian trail. It was an animal trail. We saw deer drinking. And we even saw a bear! I don't know what kind it was, because it lumbered away before we got close enough to see. But I know this: It was a big bear. Maybe a grizzly?

Next time, Charlie said he'll take his gun. I told him we shouldn't try and take down a bear. If you don't kill the bear on the first shot, it can kill you. And Charlie would need a lot more than the bird shot he had in his rifle.

November 3

This morning, I asked Ma if I could have a gun. I've only asked her about a million times. She always says no. That's because Grampa got his arm shot off in a gun accident when he was just eight years old. I've told Ma a hundred thousand times that I'm not Grampa. And I'm not eight years old, I'm nine already. She still won't let me. Today, she didn't even bother to answer. Pa didn't stick up for me, either.

November 4

This afternoon, I went and asked Grampa about getting me a gun. I reminded him how I used his gun on the trail, and how I even brought down a buffalo. But even Grampa didn't help. All he said was that I've got to be patient. "It's hard enough for your Ma to let you go into the woods," he said. "This isn't the time to be scaring her half to death about guns."

I don't see why not. Charlie's three months younger than me, and he's been hunting for two whole years.

Later

After our work was done today, Charlie and I went exploring again. We saw a fawn lying among the ferns. She didn't leap away as we got close. She just watched us, so calm-like. It would have been easy to shoot her. But even though we'd all like fresh meat, for some reason, it didn't seem fair to kill her. Maybe because she was looking at us so sweet-like. Anyway, we walked carefully so we wouldn't scare her. Then we followed the river up into the deep woods. It's real rough and wild there. And so silent. I wish like anything I had a horse so we could explore even more. But back in Missouri, we traded Pa's horses for mules and oxen to pull the wagon. I did have my own horse in Missouri, though it wasn't much of a horse. It was really just a little pony because Ma said I was too little for a full-sized horse. I could ask Grampa for a loan of his horse, Daisy. But Ma would probably say no to that, too.

November 5

Before we left Missouri, Grampa used to make fun of Pa for his reading. *Too much education, and not enough common sense.* That's what Grampa used to say about Pa.

But lots of times lately, I've found Grampa

reading to Miss Emmaline. Like today. Charlie and I were heading into the woods. We passed Grampa by the river, a book in his hand, reading aloud to Miss Emmaline. Miss Emmaline had her dress spread out all pretty around her. The sun was making a little circle of light on her hair. I guess I can see why Grampa has taken a shine to her. When he saw us, he called out, "Going exploring?"

I nodded.

Grampa looked from me to Miss Emmaline, and then back to his book. And then he looked up at me again. I had a feeling he wanted to come with us.

November 6

Raining again. Both rivers, either side of our camping land, are swollen. Pa says we may have to move to higher ground. Higher ground? I can't bear the thought of hitching up the wagon and taking down our tent, and packing up again.

But we're getting ready, just in case.

November 7

Still raining. More of our men have abandoned camp and set off for California. They say they'll come back in the spring — rich! I keep thinking we should go, too. I even think I could go alone. Well, not really alone, but go with some of the men. Ma and Pa and Becky could stay and I could come back in the spring — with gold for them!

I wonder if Grampa would go with me. But he probably wouldn't leave Miss Emmaline.

November 8

Just a hint of sun through the clouds today. But, at least, it's not pouring down rain. Pa and Uncle Arthur went out to check our land. They want to see how the valley is with all this rain. They came back and said it was good — not flooded.

Ma seems irritable and tired again. I think we're all suffering from too much rain. And too little sun.

November 9

Still misty, but the rain has let up. The rivers don't seem so swollen. Pa says we'll stay put — for now. But everybody is feeling mean. It's cold now. Pa's fingers are swollen with the cold and damp. Some mornings, I watch him rubbing them to take out the stiffness. I keep looking at my hands, wondering if they'll get all swolled up, too. So far, they look all right.

November 10

It's late and Ma says I have to blow out this candle. I begged for just one more minute, so I'll write fast. This is what happened today. Charlie and I went into the woods. Charlie had his gun. We were looking for rabbits or squirrels, or maybe even that deer that we didn't shoot the other day. I thought fresh meat might perk Ma up some. We were just a little ways over the hill, when we saw a big rabbit. Charlie shot at it. He didn't bring it down, but we could see it was wounded the way it went lopping along all zigzag. We went a long ways, trailing it. We crossed a creek, and climbed over a huge, fallen tree. It got darker and wetter the farther in we went. Then, just when we were about to give up — there was the rabbit. We almost tripped over it, lying there dead. We picked it up and started back. But we'd been so busy following that old rabbit that we hadn't noticed our path.

Suddenly, I looked at Charlie.

He looked at me. His eyes were wider than that dead rabbit's.

We didn't say a word. But we both knew: We were lost.

More tomorrow. Ma says my minute is up.

Morning, November 11

For a long time, Charlie and I stood looking around us. I looked up at the sky to get some bearings. But the timber was so tall, I couldn't see a thing. I was ashamed to be as frightened as I was. Then I remembered: We had crossed a creek while chasing the rabbit. And there was a creek meandering by to our right. I figured if we followed it, we'd be lucky and it would lead us back. Of course, it could lead us farther away, too. But we had to do something. So we set out, following it downstream. We walked for about half an hour. And then, sure enough we made a discovery. We saw the fallen tree we had climbed over. We saw the place where we had shot the rabbit.

I grinned at Charlie and he at me. We were home. Home! And best of all, I'd done it! I'd used my head, just like Grampa says to do.

And Ma and Pa were never any the wiser.

Later

Today, Charlie said he wasn't scared when we got lost. I didn't argue none. But he sure looked scared to me. I said I wasn't scared, either. Which wasn't true. At least, I was not as scared as I was when I got lost on the trail. Then, the wagons kept on moving, and they didn't even know they'd left me behind.

So then I began to think: What do you do if you get lost, really lost, and don't get lucky the way we did this time?

I thought about Charlie's gun. I bet if we didn't show up in camp by dark, all we'd have to do was shoot off the rifle. Someone would hear and come looking. That was another reason I needed a gun! But it wouldn't do to tell Ma that. And then I figured that Charlie and I had fresh rabbit meat and I sure knew by now how to build a fire. So that was my plan. And it would have worked, too — unless we met up with a grizzly.

And then I thought of something that made me grin: Even a grizzly wasn't as scary as Ma — if she ever found out I'd got lost.

November 12

Something awful happened today. Charlie and I went with the men again to work at clearing land. All the men have banded together to help one another — those who haven't left for the gold fields, that is. Today was the day to work on Mr. Hull's land. But it's so slow-going. The oxen still are weak and need to rest. But we need them to pull out the roots of the trees. And the ground is so wet, that some days, we just spend the whole time slipping and sliding in the mud. Today, Mr. Hull slipped in the mud just as a big tree was coming down. The tree didn't fall right on him. But it hit him a kind of sliding blow on the side of his head. He just crumpled down like a steer had thrown him. We all rushed to him, lying folded up there on the ground. Pa straightened him out real gentle-like. Blood was coming out of his mouth and his ears. After a bit, Mr. Hull opened his eyes. He looked around like he was wondering what he was doing lying there. And then he said, "Take care of my little ones." He sighed. He closed his eyes. And he was gone!

He has ten little ones. And I'd thought our bad times would be over once we got to Oregon.

Later

Back at camp, all the women gathered around Mrs. Hull. When they brought in her dead husband's body, she just stood there looking down at him. She clutched both her hands together and rocked herself back and forth. All her children gathered around. The littlest ones held on to her skirt. Nobody spoke. They didn't even cry at first. It was like everything went real still for a few minutes. Like there was nothing worth saying, anyway.

Now the men are digging a burial place for him.

November 13

Funny how people are. On the trail, Mrs. Gibbons's husband got killed. Mrs. Gibbons was so tore up, she couldn't do a thing for herself or her two babies. She couldn't cook a meal. She couldn't look after her little ones. Nothing. All she could do was cry. So Mrs. Hull took her in along with her own ten babies, took care of the whole lot of them. She treated them just like they were some of her own children.

And now, with Mr. Hull gone, Mrs. Gibbons is caring for the Hulls. She cooks and chases after the little ones. I even saw her take a stick to Frederick's behind when he sassed his ma.

Pa says you never know what people can really do till they have to do it.

November 14

More worries. As the rain keeps up, the ground is more and more wet. Now, building and clearing has stopped completely. Poor Ma. We'll never be in a house by Christmas.

Folks just hide out in their tents and there's hardly any visiting. Only time we came together this week was to bury Mr. Hull.

November 15

Last night, I pretended to be asleep in my sleeping roll, but I heard Ma and Pa by the fire, talking. They're worrying over things now.

Money is a worry. Most of ours has run out, Pa said. And while hunting and fishing can bring us food, we need other things. Supplies, nails, roofing materials. I heard Pa say he might look for work for a while.

Ma got this real scared sound in her voice. She said, "Not the gold mines, Mr. McCullough!"

"Not the mines," Pa said softly. But then he added that he could work in Oregon City. Storekeepers there need lots of help, he said. The city is almost emptied out of men because of everyone rushing to California.

Ma didn't say anything to that. I don't know what she thinks.

But I know what I think. I went to sleep with my heart sad. We came to Oregon for Pa — for him to work the land. Out of doors, the way he loves. We didn't come all the way to Oregon for Pa to work in a store.

November 16

This morning, Grampa came riding up to our tent on his horse, Daisy. Grampa has only one arm, but he rides better than almost anybody. He talked quietly to Pa for a while. Pa grinned and nodded. From the quiet way they were talking, I knew they didn't want Ma to hear. Or maybe it was me they were keeping secrets from. After a bit, Grampa rode off. He waved at me, and he grinned. That was all. But his grin told me that something was up.

Something *is* up. Pa told me to be ready to go with Grampa early tomorrow. He didn't say where. He didn't say for what. He just said be ready early. And then he said, real soft-like, "And don't tell your ma."

I'm tucking my diary in my pack and will be ready before the sun is even up.

November 17

I'm in Oregon City. I'm sitting on a bench in front of a bank, looking at the clock up there. There's horses and wagons clanking by and people everywhere — men and women and children.

This city's even bigger and newer looking than St. Joseph, Missouri. There are rows and rows of houses, most of them side by side. They're so close together, there's hardly enough room for a man to walk sideways between them. Some of the buildings are two and three stories high. Across the street, there's a saloon with a hotel on top of it. Music is pouring out the doors. And I hear men hooting with laughter. Grampa has left me here. He says he'll be back in an hour. He still hasn't said why we've come. But I guess I don't care. There's so much to see, my eyes are just about popping out of my head.

Night

We're back home, and I'm so tired I can hardly hold this pencil. But I have to tell this: I have a horse. My very own horse. Grampa bought him for me. More tomorrow. I need to blow out the candle. And sleep.

Morning, November 18

This is what happened. When Grampa came back, we rode out to a ranch, where there were a couple dozen horses in a corral. Grampa and I were walking around the corral, when a stranger appeared in front of us. His legs were all bowed out, like he'd been riding a horse his whole life.

He said something to Grampa — I think in French. There's plenty of trappers down from Canada, and I've heard them talk. Somehow, with bits of English and French, and lots of grunts, they seemed to understand each other. They shook hands. And I guess they had worked out some sort of bargain. The long and short of it was this: When they were finished talking — I had myself a horse. I rode him all the way home, just talking and talking to him. He kept his ears laid back, like he was listening to my every word. He's a black-and-white gelding with the sweetest disposition you can imagine.

I've named him Hurricane.

November 19

I've been a little shy with Ma for the last two days. I can tell she's just furious with Pa and Grampa for letting me have a horse — a real horse. And a gelding, at that. And maybe she's furious with me, too. So I'm lying real low, and every time Ma looks at me, I try to grin.

She doesn't grin back. But today she looked at me for a long, long time. And then she put a hand on my head. She said, "Just try not to break your neck." She didn't exactly smile, but it was soft the way she said it.

So then I knew it was going to be all right. I hurried right out to the pasture to tell Hurricane.

November 20

With all the excitement about my horse, I forgot to tell this: While we were in Oregon City, Grampa got a newspaper. It's called the *Oregon Spectator,* and we brought it back here. Now, everybody is passing it around, talking about the news. The biggest news is what happened in August while we were still on the trail — crossing mountains probably. It says that on August 14, Oregon became a territory of the United States. But what has everybody talking, is not that it's just a territory. It's a *non-slave* territory. That means no one here can hold or own slaves. I'm very glad of that. Pa's glad, too. He says it's one reason he's happy we left Missouri. And Grampa says it's shameful for one person to own another person, buying and selling them like cattle.

But some of the people here are not so happy. I heard Mr. West say that he was thinking of moving on again — to some place where a decent man could own a decent slave.

Ma looked right at Mr. West. She said, "I don't see how owning a slave can be decent."

Sometimes, I think Ma should have been born a man.

November 21

Today, Grampa and I rode out to see our land. It was pouring rain, so there was no work going on. We just sat there on our horses, looking over the hillside. Looking down on the valley, I couldn't help thinking how pretty it was. I asked Hurricane if he agreed. He flicked his ears back and forth. I figured that meant he was saying yes.

And then I thought of what Ma had said — that Grampa had his own plans for his house. "Where will you build?" I asked. "Near us?"

Grampa shook his head. "Miss Emmaline's too delicate for this kind of living," he said. "We're taking ourselves to Oregon City." He clucked at Daisy, dug in his heels, and turned her toward home.

Oregon City! But that was so far!

"And don't tell your ma," Grampa shouted over his shoulder. "Not yet."

But from the way Ma had screwed up her face that night, I had a feeling she already knew.

Later

Grampa's always near. Even though he's married and I don't see him every minute the way I used to — he's always here. I can count on it. But living in Oregon City? I hated that! All the way back home on Hurricane, I thought of arguments, reasons why he had to stay here. When we got home and dismounted, we began walking our horses, cooling them down. And I told Grampa all my arguments. I ended with the biggest argument of all: He'd be too far. And I wouldn't see him hardly at all.

Grampa just turned and grinned at me. He stopped walking and leaned across my horse. "Josh, boy," he said, real soft-like. "Why in tarnation do you think I bought you a horse?"

November 22

Folks here are passing the newspaper hand to hand, gathering around and reading and talking. The paper is so torn up and wet, you can hardly read the words anymore. But there's so much news. Senator Hart Benton, our senator from back in Missouri, he's the one who got the bill passed — the one that said no slaves in the territory. Strange, because Missouri has slaves. But maybe Senator Benton has started to feel different about whether that's right or not.

It's on my mind a lot now. I think of how Grampa bought Hurricane for me. Imagine buying a man just like you buy a horse!

November 23

More rain. Still no more work on our house. And now, we worry about flooding. The campgrounds get smaller each day as the water creeps up. We're packed and ready to flee. But where? Grampa came by last night and said we should go to Oregon City.

Pa said maybe. Ma just shook her head.

And to think that I believed our worries would be over once we got here. I think maybe we all believed that.

Night

Tonight, some men in camp got into a fight. And can you believe — they were fighting over slavery?! Nobody knows just who said what to start it. At first, there were just two men fighting, slipping and sliding in the mud. But then, before you knew it, there were about a dozen. Some men were trying to hold back other men. Finally, Pa and Uncle Arthur got the men separated. And everybody seemed to calm down some. But wouldn't you know? At the bottom of the pile, the one who started it, was Mr. West. He was still growling at someone as Pa led him back to his tent. He was promising to get even. He said next time, he'd fight till there was a funeral. Pa says if he doesn't get some sense in his head, it'll be his own funeral.

November 24

In the paper, there's a story about two senators getting into a fight. They started a fistfight on the floor of the Senate, fighting over slavery. One was the Missouri senator, Senator

Hart Benton, and the other, Senator Andrew Butler of South Carolina. One called the other a liar, and then Senator Benton said almost the same exact words as Mr. West said. He said they'd fight again. "But take notice, sir, that when I fight, I fight for a funeral."

I wonder if a senator would really kill another man. I think not. But I'm not so sure what Mr. West would do.

Later

Tonight, more quiet, fretful talk between Ma and Pa. The way Pa paced up and down in front of our tent, I could see he was all upset, something he hardly ever is. Ma was working on soothing him down. But I could tell she was upset and worried, too.

I'm worried. If only we could get into a

house, we'd all be better. There must be something we can do. There must be something that *I* can do.

November 25

Today, I met Frederick Hull on the green. He says he hasn't told his ma, but he's going to sneak off to California. There's gold everywhere there, he says. It's just lying in the creeks. All you have to do is put down a sifter, and there it is — a pan full of gold.

He says he has to help his ma somehow, now that his pa is dead.

November 26

Me and Charlie have been talking about gold. If what everyone says is true, maybe we should go to California. Charlie says it doesn't take long to get there. I know Pa thinks it's foolish. But maybe Pa is wrong. I think I'll ask Grampa.

Later

I've been looking at Ma and looking at Ma, and looking at her. She looks different somehow. And today, I figured it out! I think she's going to have a baby.

I'm so happy for her. And scared, too. What if this baby dies like the others? And something else: Maybe this is why Pa's so worried. Another mouth to feed.

I wonder if I should say anything about what I noticed.

I think not.

November 27

There's been a bit of a dry spell, so the men are working on clearing land again. Some of the lots, like ours, are almost cleared. And now we're splitting trees into lumber.

It's hard work. I keep looking at my hands. They're so callused they look like a man's hands. But it's good to be working again. I can see just where our house will be.

Night

Tonight at supper, Pa said he's planning a trip to Oregon City for supplies. Ma nodded but she didn't say anything.

I suspect she's wondering if that's the real reason he's going. Or if he's aiming to get himself a job. I can't bear the thought of Pa working in a store or a bank.

But none of us said anything more. We finished our supper in silence.

November 28

When I saw Frederick Hull this morning, I asked him when he was leaving for California. He said soon. And then he squinted up his eyes at me. "You're not fixing to tell, are you?!" he said.

I told him I wasn't fixing to tell. But I didn't tell him that maybe I was fixing to go with him.

Later

Tonight, I told Grampa what I was thinking about California. Grampa put his arm around my shoulder. He walked me out to the wagon, then leaned on one wheel.

"Son," he said. "I'll be the first to admit — when we first started out, I thought your pa was a fool. But I was wrong. It weren't foolish. Oregon's a real fine place to be."

"But there's gold in California," I said. "*Gold.*"

Grampa squinted up his eyes at me. "Josh, boy," he said. "Use your head. There's some things worth risking a life for. Only a fool risks his life for gold."

Later still

Tonight at supper, Ma was fussing at me and fussing at me. Seems she thinks I've got no manners anymore. She doesn't like the way I eat. She doesn't like the way I talk. She says my speech has gotten all rough. I don't see what's so different about it. I never say "ain't," the word Ma hates most in the whole world.

And at the table, well, sometimes I do forget and use my sleeve to wipe my mouth. I told her I'd try to do better. But how can I remember to do all those nice things? We're still living in a tent.

November 29

Tonight, Becky came running out on to the green when I came up on Hurricane. She begged for a ride. I pulled her up and put my arms around her skinny little waist. Suddenly, holding her like that, my heart jumped up into my throat, this scared feeling. It just seems it's awful easy for children to die out here. And she's so tiny, her bones are like bird bones. I held her carefully and made Hurricane trot real slow all around the green. After a bit, I looked up and saw Ma standing outside our tent. She had her arms folded. Uh-oh. At first,

I thought she was mad. But when we got closer, I saw she was smiling. I stopped in front of her and slid Becky down. And then, I climbed down and held the reins for Ma. "Can I offer you a ride, Mrs. McCullough?" I said.

Ma just swatted at my bottom with a dishrag. But she was grinning.

If I only knew how to keep her smiling.

Later

Pa spent all of this morning oiling the cover of our wagon to make it more waterproof. It's been raining hard again almost every day now. Pa says we can move back into the wagon if he can make it more waterproof. The tent leaks like a miner's sieve. I don't even try and find a dry place to sleep anymore. I just lie down and close my eyes, and hope I won't wake up drowned.

November 30

This morning, Pa took the wagon and went to Oregon City with Uncle Arthur and Grampa. When they came back, Grampa was grinning. Nobody's said anything yet. But I know something has happened. I told Charlie I thought maybe Grampa has found a house for him and Miss Emmaline. We both hope so. We hope maybe they'll invite us to come visit. And stay overnight.

I'm beginning to feel like Ma. I wouldn't mind sleeping in a house for a change.

Later

It's pouring today. It's been raining for a week and the rivers are rising. The whole green is flooded. Pa and I moved everything from the tent into the wagon. It's more waterproof and we're a bit drier inside. But still, there's water everywhere. We're all ready to move out if need be. If the rivers rise, all we have to do is hitch up the oxen and get Hurricane and Buster, and Laurie, too.

I wonder just how bad the rising water is. Pa seems real somber.

December 1

Winter. And cold. And damp!

It started out a terrible day. And got worse. First, the rain. Then the rising river. Then, Becky fell off the back of the wagon and twisted up her ankle and it's swolled up. And Ma scolded me for not watching her better! Then, to top it all, Aunt Lizzie is acting like she's about to have her baby. Ma is about crazed with trying to set things up for birthing. But she can't even get a fire going in this rain.

We think we might drive to Oregon City with Aunt Lizzie. Folks there are known to open their houses to strangers in need. I think Aunt Lizzie is in real need. Right now, she's sitting in the middle of our wagon, just about doubled over with pain. But she doesn't want to go into the city. She says the jolting wagon would be even worse. Besides, she says she's not hurting that much.

It hurts me just watching her hurting.

Night

Aunt Lizzie refuses to budge. So we're staying put for now. Ma has chased me out of the wagon. She sent me and Becky to sit with Charlie in his wagon. Adam West came and sat with us, too. He hardly ever joins up with us anymore. His Pa keeps him close to his own tent. But tonight, his Pa has gone off to town,

I think. To pass the time, the three of us began telling ghost stories. Adam told a really creepy tale about a boy being followed by a ghost wolf. But I forgot that Becky was listening. She suddenly began to sob and shiver. She said she'd seen a ghost creep under the flap of the wagon. It had orange teeth and whiskers. I told her ghosts don't have whiskers. And they don't have orange teeth because they don't have any teeth. That made her cry even more. But now I've soothed her to sleep. Charlie and Adam and I are just sitting listening. Every few minutes we hear a cry — like the call of a wolf or a coyote. But we know it's Aunt Lizzie. I'm awful glad I'm not a woman.

Morning, December 2

A baby is born, a little girl baby! And Aunt Lizzie seems to have survived it all just fine.

This morning, she's sitting up in the wagon, taking congratulations from all the women. The men are more shy. But Uncle Arthur is real pleased, you can tell.

Even old Mrs. Meaney hobbled over to say how-do. She brought some more of that stuff she's always knitting — a shawl, this time, I think. I know Aunt Lizzie was happy to have it, to wrap herself and the baby. I think she gave birth in the wettest birthing bed anyone has ever had. It's still pouring down rain today.

Later

Ma told me the new baby's name. It will be Isabel. I'm glad it's a girl because of Rachel dying. I think the new baby will be very loved. When I said that to Ma, she surprised me by reaching out and hugging me. Baby Isabel is so little — I've never seen such a tiny baby. I saw

Ma go to put a diaper on it, and its little bottom could fit in the palm of my hand. Funny to think it will someday grow into a full-sized person. I hope.

December 3

Flood! We're throwing things in the wagons. I've hitched up Hurricane and Laurie, our cow, and put Buster in the wagon with us. We're heading out. More later.

Later

We've been riding all through the night. Miss Emmaline's in the wagon with us. Grampa's riding Daisy. Aunt Lizzie and Charlie are in the wagon right behind. And there's about another dozen wagons behind them. Some folks wouldn't come, though. They decided to stay and wait out the storm. I'm glad we've left. It's so black, and the water's rising so fast. Our oxen have to swim at times. My heart is thundering in my throat. Nobody says anything. I think we're all praying.

Late night

Flashes of lightning light up the sky. Trees have been thrown down and are in our way. One of our oxen tripped and fell. It took a long while to get him up again. We're heading for Oregon City. It's high ground, Pa says.

I pray that we'll make it.

December 4

Morning. But still it's almost black as night. There's water everywhere, right up through the bottom of our wagon. Kettles and pans and blankets float and slosh around inside. Everything's covered with mud. Rain lashes at us in sheets. Outside the wagons, I can see Pa and Uncle Arthur and Grampa huddled together. Pa points this way. Grampa points another. I wonder what they're deciding.

About an hour later

Grampa came back to whisper to Miss Emmaline. She nodded and touched his hand. She hasn't said much, but I can see she's scared silly. Who isn't? Grampa looked at me then. He tilted his head toward Miss Emmaline. It was like he was asking me to take care of her.

I nodded at him.

And then he was gone.

Same day, still pouring down rain

Pa came and stood at the back of our wagon. He says he thinks we're lost. Did we get turned around in the dark? Are we heading back to Abernathy Green and the rising rivers? We don't know. We can hear a river roaring in front of us. Pa says we mustn't rush on farther. We'll take a rest and see if with more morning light, we can figure where we are. And if it's safe to try and ford the river that we hear in front of us.

Becky began to whimper.

I pulled her into my lap and hugged her close. It's about the only thing I know to do right now.

December 5

Still waiting for light.

I've given some feed to Hurricane and tried

to milk Laurie. Laurie didn't give much. I think she's wore out. Ma has gone to help Aunt Lizzie with the baby. Grampa stops and visits with Miss Emmaline. I'm making shadows with the lantern on the wagon cover for Becky. I used my hand to make a rabbit shadow. Then I made a dog with its mouth opening and closing. It made Becky laugh. Miss Emmaline laughed, too. Grampa just watched me, smiling.

We've got nothing to do now but wait. And pray.

Later

It's a little lighter. Sometimes it seems the storm has let up a bit. And then it tumbles down sheets of rain. But Pa and Grampa and Uncle Arthur have agreed on direction.

We hope it's the right direction.

Late

A whole day of riding through the hardest rain I have ever seen. There was an awful bad storm on the trail once with hail and everything. That seems like a gentle spring storm compared to this.

But Pa says he thinks we'll be there soon. To think — Grampa and I rode Daisy into Oregon City in an hour or two. This trip has taken more than an entire day.

Even later

We're here in Oregon City. Grampa knows some folks who will put us up a while. So now he's left us, ridden off on Daisy. Our wagons are gathered at the end of a wide street. Pa says we'll just sit and wait. If need be, we can live in our wagons right here a while. We might be wet, but at least we won't drown. Only worry is this: The Hulls' wagon that started out with us hasn't gotten here. We're a bit worried. We wonder if they got lost. Or did they maybe turn back and get overrun by water? It's still pouring down rain.

Night

Grampa came back, gave a signal, and our wagons started up along the main street. We passed the bank and the saloon and the hotel, all those places I saw when I was here with Grampa. Folks came out of their houses, some still in their nightshirts, to look at us coming down the main street like a parade. But they must be the friendliest folks ever. Because now, each of our wagons has a new family — a home, people to live with till things dry out. Ma and Pa and Becky and Buster and me, we'll stay in a house owned by Mr. Mott. He's a banker here in town. His wife and daughters are a bit shy. But they treat us so good. And Mr. Mott is so respectful. He acts like maybe Pa were President Polk himself.

Around midnight

I'm lying in a bed, a candle by my side. I'm actually dry. I'm warm. I'm inside a house. It's been six months since I've slept in a bed in a house. Becky is alongside me. Ma and Pa have another bed in this room. Miss Emmaline's staying here, too. But she'll sleep in a different room. Nobody's sleeping yet, though. Ma's in the kitchen, talking with Mrs. Mott. Pa and Grampa have gone out. They took Daisy and Hurricane and went back to check on the Hulls. Pa says we need to look out for them extra special since there's no man with them.

I begged to go, too. But as usual, Ma said no.

I turned to Grampa for help. But Ma was glaring.

Grampa just patted my shoulder. "Take care of your ma," he said softly. "She needs you, too." And then he grinned at me. "Besides, you got a lot to record in that journal of yours. Tell it all — the good and the not-so-good."

And then he was gone.

I hope the Hulls are all right. I think they probably are. They've come two thousand miles already. There's not much that can beat you down after you've done that.

December 6

Morning light. No rain! Sun is peeking through the window. Becky's sleeping beside me, her doll tucked under her head. She has her arms and legs flung out, like she's a doll herself.

Ma's sleeping, too. But no Pa. I guess he's

still out with Grampa. I wonder if they found the Hulls. And where.

I wish I could have gone to help.

Later

My hands are shaking so, I can hardly hold this pencil. Someone came thundering down the street on a horse. He was shouting about an overturned wagon. And a body in the river. A body, he was yelling. And a drowned horse.

We've thrown on clothes and are gathered in the yard in front of the house.

Ma's face couldn't be whiter than if she'd seen a ghost.

Still waiting

And waiting. The sun is up. Some men have saddled up. They brought a horse for

Uncle Arthur. They're all going back looking to help.

But if it's true that someone is dead — who is it?

I can't bear to think.

More waiting

I keep praying to God — not Grampa, not Pa. Please, God, not either one of them. Maybe it's one of the Hulls. Or the Gibbons. But not Pa. Not Grampa. I know maybe that's the wrong kind of prayer to pray. But I can't help it. And I can't help praying this, either: Don't let the drowned horse be Hurricane.

Noon almost

The sun's straight overhead.

Finally, far down the street, I see something.

It's a wagon! It's covered in mud, with just two oxen. Beside it are men — men on horseback. Pa? Grampa? I can't see.

We're all crowded out to the edge of the wooden sidewalk. Becky is clinging to Ma's skirt. No one makes a sound. I still can't see. But — I see a horse. A horse with something — a body? — lying across its back. My horse, Hurricane.

Oh, God, oh, is that Pa? Please, God, no! Please don't let it be Pa.

Much, much later

Pa's here. He's been holding me to him. I'm trying to be a man. But tears are wetting this page.

Grampa. My grampa is dead.

Night

Grampa is dead. If I write it enough, will it be real?

Nothing feels real.

Grampa is dead.

Later

Ma's walking around like she's been hit broadside with something. Becky is whiny and clings to Ma. Miss Emmaline looks like she's half dead herself, so white and still. Pa's trying to help everyone, even though he got hurt himself. He's limping something bad. Seems they were trying to right the wagon that got overturned in the river. Somehow Grampa got caught underneath. Pa says he and Frederick Hull worked like anything to free Grampa. But it didn't do any good. By the time they got

Grampa pulled out — he was drowned. He was dead.

He *is* dead.

Inside my head, I thought — if I had been there, I could have saved him.

Pa turned to me. It was like he was reading my mind. Real soft-like, he said, "Son, that wagon weighs a couple of tons. Only God Himself could have moved it faster than we did."

Morning, December 7

We'll have a funeral for Grampa tomorrow. It's going to be in a church. A real church. And he'll get buried in a graveyard. I heard Aunt Lizzie tell Ma that at least he won't get buried on the prairie for wolves to dig up.

It made me sick to think.

I went out in the backyard and threw up.

Later

I'm supposed to be a man. I keep writing here that I feel all grown up. Now I don't feel grown up. I feel like crying.

Morning, December 8

Ma and Aunt Lizzie keep saying it was the most beautiful funeral ever. How can a funeral be beautiful? Grampa lay still and white in that coffin box. Miss Emmaline and Charlie and me — we just stood and looked and looked at him. Once, I thought he was breathing. I held my breath, trying to see — was he? Or was it just that when I breathed, he seemed to breathe? I went and touched his hand. He was dead.

Later, at the Motts' house

That church was packed full, even though we hardly know a soul in this whole town. Folks came up and tried to comfort us. And we were offered help and a place to stay. Afterwards, Ma turned to Pa. She said she never knew folks could be so kind. It did me good to hear her say that because I know Pa's feeling awful bad. I figure I know what he's thinking. Because I'm thinking it, too: *If we'd stayed in Missouri, Grampa would still be alive*.

Later, still at the Motts' house

We're going to stay here for a while. The Motts have insisted. I can tell Pa doesn't like the idea. But there's talk of disease back in the campground. And Aunt Lizzie is staying right across the street for a while. I guess Ma gave in because of the baby swelling inside her. I know how she prays for a healthy baby.

Pa says there's one good thing about the flood — it floated up a small purse from between the boards of our wagon. Pa thought the purse had been lost on the trail. There were enough gold coins in it to buy some provisions we need.

I wonder if it's enough to keep us till spring. Or if Pa will have to work in town.

I wonder if it matters.

Still at the Motts' house, December 9

The river waters have gone down some, so today Pa and Uncle Arthur went to the campground. They came back here tonight. They said they spent all day digging graves for people who drowned. One of the dead is Adam

West. Adam? I can hardly believe it. He was telling us a ghost story just the other night.

He was just nine years old.

Later

Tonight, I heard Ma tell Pa that Mr. Mott would give him a job in the bank anytime he wanted.

Pa didn't answer.

Morning, early, by candlelight, December 10

Today I'm going with the men back to the green to help. Pa says our first job is to get the mud cleaned up. Then we'll start rebuilding. He says there'll be no more building houses till spring. But there's plenty of timber knocked down by the flood to build other things. Folks will need lean-tos and new platforms for tents and such.

That's Pa's way. Always thinking how to help others.

Morning and cold

Ice is everywhere.

When we got to Abernathy Green, I could hardly believe it was the place we'd left. The green isn't green anymore. It's mud, thick slippery mud, with a coating of ice on top. If you take just a step or two, you have to stop and scrape mud off your shoe bottoms, six inches thick about. Trees got swept away. Covered wagons are all overturned and tattered and torn.

I looked where Grampa's tent used to be. All that was left was a bedroll and a flap of the tent wedged between two trees. I dug down into the mud, to see if there was anything else. I found three books. They're all soaked and mud-caked. But I took all three and put them in the wagon for Miss Emmaline.

We spent all day shoveling mud and laying down planks. We'll use them as a platform for some lean-tos.

At noon, Mrs. Meaney called us all to her tent. She had cooked up a bean soup for everyone.

I don't know why — but it always surprises me what people do to help other people. And I think of how Grampa died trying to do just that.

Later

Every time Pa looks at me, I try to grin. I don't know if I'm fooling him none though. I think my red eyes give me away.

Next morning, December 12

Today, on the way to the green, I asked Pa, "Why are we just fixing platforms and lean-tos? Why don't we work on our house? Our land is clear."

"Not yet," Pa said. "Come spring."

"But there's lots of timber around," I said. Pa shook his head. "It's too wet," he said. "The lumber's wet, the ground is wet."

"So?" I said. "We'll use wet lumber. It needn't be fancy. Just a little tiny house. A cabin."

Pa looked at me for a long time. He just shook his head.

"Ma really needs a house," I said.

Later

All day, as we worked side by side, I kept thinking about the house. We needed a house. We really needed it.

It'll make all the difference, Pa. It's what we came for, Pa. Land. A home. We didn't come all the way to Oregon so you could work in a bank. We didn't come for Ma to live in somebody else's house.

It doesn't have to be fancy. A little cabin will do.

I didn't say those things out loud. Just inside my head.

But maybe Pa heard. Because coming home in the wagon, Uncle Arthur turned to Pa. "What do you think of Josh's idea?" he said. "We could build a cabin. And add on more come spring."

And then Pa surprised me. He said, "We'll see."

Days later, but I don't know what day

At night, I'm too tired to write. Most nights, we just bed down here at the campground, sleeping right in the open. Other nights we ride back into town. We're working hard. More later.

Another day

Ma asked me last night why I'm so quiet lately. I couldn't tell her the truth. Truth is, I'm scared that if I open my mouth, I'll tell. I'll tell about our house. Now, I've got to blow out the candle and sleep. Tomorrow's another work day.

Morning

I've been so tired, I couldn't write here. But I remember Grampa telling me — *Record it, Josh.*

So I'll try to catch up here. For weeks, we've been working on our house. Everybody's helping everybody, so the work goes fast. It's not fancy. It's just a cabin. But it's ours. And it's almost ready. It's for Charlie's family and ours together, just like our mamas hoped for. We even curtained off a corner for Miss Emmaline to have a private place. We haven't told Ma or Aunt Lizzie or Miss Emmaline what we're doing — not yet. It's our secret.

It'll be ready in about a week we think. In time for Christmas.

Almost Christmas

We've not only built our house. Charlie and me, we made a table and some little stools. Pa and Uncle Arthur built a fireplace inside. They've even outfitted the house with some new pots and plates. Last night, Pa sneaked off into town and bought a featherbed for Ma and one for Aunt Lizzie.

We're helping the Hulls build a cabin, too. Frederick Hull hasn't run off to California. Instead, he's working as hard as any man to build a house for his family. Even his ma and sisters pitch in.

Everyone is helping everyone. Mr. West, the meanest man I know, seems to have gotten a bit kinder. He spent all day today, side by side with Pa, laying out a sort of road between our house and the green. It'll make it easier, getting the wagons in and out. And it will be easier for walking from house to house. And he spent another whole day, yesterday, up on our roof, putting in nails. I wanted to tell him I was sorry about his son. But I didn't know how to say it. I hope he knows.

Even closer to Christmas

Today is our last day of getting ready. We've told Ma and Aunt Lizzie and Miss Emmaline that we have a surprise for them tomorrow. I wonder if they suspect.

I know Ma will be real happy. A house. Her own house. I just hope it's fancy enough. I'm scared that she's been getting awful spoiled in Oregon City.

Christmas Eve

Ma was so happy when she saw our house, that she just stood there grinning and grinning, and not saying anything. And Aunt Lizzie was so happy she began bouncing up and down. I had to reach out and take tiny Isabel from her arms, I was so scared she'd drop her. Even Miss Emmaline had this big broad smile on her face. And then the two of them — my mama and her twin sister — they danced! It was embarrassing, Ma with her big stomach, but — but I want to tell the truth. And that's the truth.

Ma and Aunt Lizzie were dancing, kicking up their heels. All the women came out of their lean-tos and wagons, all came out to watch. And before you knew it, others joined in, laughing and just twirling around on these wooden planks like they was on a stage or something. Even Miss Emmaline took a step or two.

The men just stood there, arms folded, watching and shaking their heads like they were watching some mad women. But you could tell the men were so proud, they could hardly stand still themselves.

Ma saw me standing there holding Baby Isabel, and she grabbed me in her arms and hugged me. And then, she and Aunt Lizzie, too — they both bust out crying. But I'm used to that by now and it didn't scare me none. Women cry when they get happy.

Christmas Night

There's a fire in the fireplace. The whole house smells of pine boughs and pies baking. There's candles in the window — yes, we've got one window in front. And there's a bed in the corner, with a trundle under it, laid out with straw and pine boughs for a mattress. That's where me and Becky will sleep. In the corner is a cradle. Mrs. Hull brought it with her from St. Joseph. She said she won't be needing it no more, so Ma can have it. I think our new baby will come pretty soon.

Folks are walking carefully on the planks, coming to visit. Ma has enough food to serve everyone in town, seems like. She and Aunt Lizzie and Miss Emmaline have been baking the whole two days we've been here. And all the other ladies have been baking and sharing, too. I think Ma is just so happy to have a place to call her own. I'm glad Pa agreed that we shouldn't wait for spring. Some things are too important to wait for.

April 1, 1849

It's been a long time since I've written here. I'm just too tired at night to even hold a pencil. Days are longer and warmer, and we're busy planting and building and clearing and adding to our house.

But best of all, now that it's spring, the sun shines most every day. Well, at least a part of every day.

April 9

Today, I saw Becky go running on to the green just as a wagon was rolling up — rolling way too fast. I reached for her, and quick scooped her out of the way. And then, I turned her upside down, and paddled her little bottom. She burst into tears, and I felt bad. But it was just that I was so scared for her. I saw then that Pa was watching. He came and put a hand on my arm. He said that I'm growing into a real man.

I had to turn away, because I suddenly felt shy. But I felt my chest swell up like anything.

April 10

A whole year has passed since we left St. Joseph. I think of all that has happened. I think of the last thing Grampa said to me: *Tell it all, Josh, the good and the not-so-good.* I'm afraid I've been mostly telling the not-so-good. So now, it's time to tell the good.

Pa's humming again, just the way he used to. He's already planted trees, tiny seedlings, a whole orchard of trees. He's working outdoors, working the land. And he won't have to work in a store or the bank.

Ma and Aunt Lizzie are busy with the babies, and you can just see how happy they are. And oh, yes! How did I forget to record this? I have a baby brother. His name is Hector and he's the squallingest baby ever. Pa says that's because he's healthy. He's already lived two months. Ma says that means he'll live a long, long life.

Charlie and Uncle Arthur and me, we're all working on adding to our little house on the hill. And when we finish in the evenings,

Charlie and I go and explore the woods. I still don't have a gun. But I guess that's all right for now. Miss Emmaline seems healed a bit now. She spends a lot of time helping Ma with little Hector and reading to Becky. And sometimes, in the evenings, I read to them both, Becky and Miss Emmaline, too.

I'm a good brother to Becky and to Hector, too. I even have more patience with Ma. She can't help worrying, I know. I'm beginning to feel the same worrisome way with Becky, and little Hector, too, wanting to protect them from everything.

What else? Hurricane is getting stronger and wilder by the day. And me, I've shot up about three inches, and my pants don't fit at all. I've even outgrown my shoes.

And yesterday, Pa said that I was getting to be a real man.

So there's lots of good here. Lots and lots of good things here. Grampa would be glad to have me write that.

P.S. Just as I was closing up my journal, I had to open it again and record this: At sunset tonight, Pa was standing on the hill, looking over our land. He called Ma to him.

"Look, look there," Pa said, pointing to the fields. His voice was soft, and I could just tell that his heart was up there crowding his throat.

I looked where he was pointing. The sky had flared up red, then turned purple and gray and pink. Tiny fruit trees were showing tiny green buds in the distance. Our house was behind us, the walls strong, smoke from the chimney poking up into the sky. Pa had his arm around Ma's shoulder. Ma had Hector in her arms, and Becky was clinging to her skirt.

All four of them stood there close together, sort of shiny-looking in the sunset.

It made my throat feel choked, too.

And I thought again of Grampa and what he'd said that time. And I knew he was right: Oregon is a real fine place to be.

Historical Note

Many who came to the end of the Oregon Trail felt truly blessed and certain that their goals had been achieved. They had found fertile, free land — rich and dark and theirs for the taking.

A wagon train on the Oregon Trail.

The fears of the journey — starvation, attacks by Indians, accidents, river crossings, illnesses — all seemed in the past. Moreover, many felt that they had proven something to themselves: that they could face the harshest of times and survive. Thus there was a feeling of exultation and rejoicing, a sense of having found the home that they had sought.

But for many, those feelings were often short-lived. For in this promised land there were still hardships to be endured. The air was very different from what many had left behind in Missouri. Winds blew, and when rains came it rained and rained and rained. There were still Indians to contend with and to fear — and to try to make peace with. There were mud slides and dreary days spent living out of doors (in tents and covered wagons) while land was chosen and houses built. Crops had to be planted and orchards laid out. Many cumbersome household items had been

A pioneer family works to build a home.

left along the trail, and they needed to be replaced, but often the new settlers had arrived without any money left. Also, there were often squabbles among neighbors and within families who were overburdened and tired from the hardships of the trail. And there was still mourning to do, for those who had died on the trail and for family left behind in the East.

Also, there were many settlers who had come on the trail because they were restless and dissatisfied by nature. And though they had traveled so many miles, sometimes the new land did not satisfy that restless itch the way some thought it might. There was talk of going even farther — perhaps as far as Hawaii and Chile.

And then, in one terrible winter, there were the floods that swept away homes and roads and cattle — and people.

For some, this seemed even more unbearable than the trail hardships, for by now they had arrived in the Willamette Valley and should have been safe.

With a lot of hard work, a family's farm develops.

But these hardships were also weathered, for the settlers were a hardy lot. And for those who stayed and persevered, the end of the Oregon Trail was, at last, much as they had hoped for: a land of plenty, of rich soil, and of long growing seasons. A land where they could live out the dreams they had dreamed.

Life in the Oregon Territory finally gets easier.

About the Author

Patricia Hermes is the author of more than thirty books for children and young adults. She has written four other books for the My America series, *Our Strange New Land*, *The Starving Time*, and *Season of Promise*, which are the stories of Elizabeth Barker's experiences in Jamestown Colony in 1609, as well as Joshua's first diary, *Westward to Home*. Many of her books have received awards, from Children's Choice Awards to state awards, ALA Best Books, and ALA Notable Book awards.

For Benjamin Barrett Hermes

Acknowledgments

Grateful acknowledgment is made for permission to reprint the following:

Cover portrait by Glenn Harrington.

Page 101: Covered wagon train, Denver Public Library.
Page 103: "The Beginning," Starting the settlement on the American Frontier, Stock Montage, Inc.
Page 104: "The First Season," Settlers starting homesteads in the Oregon Territory, Stock Montage, Inc.
Page 105: "The settlers' first home in the Far West," drawn by W. A. Rogers. New York Public Library.

Other books in the My America series

Corey's Underground Railroad Diaries
by Sharon Dennis Wyeth
Book One: Freedom's Wings
Book Two: Flying Free

Elizabeth's Jamestown Colony Diaries
by Patricia Hermes
Book One: Our Strange New Land
Book Two: The Starving Time
Book Three: Season of Promise

Hope's Revolutionary War Diaries
by Kristiana Gregory
Book One: Five Smooth Stones
Book Two: We Are Patriots

Joshua's Oregon Trail Diaries
by Patricia Hermes
Book One: Westward to Home

Meg's Prairie Diaries
by Kate McMullan
Book One: As Far As I Can See

Virginia's Civil War Diaries
by Mary Pope Osborne
Book One: My Brother's Keeper
Book Two: After the Rain

While the events described and some of the characters in this book may be based on actual historical events and real people, Joshua McCullough is a fictional character, created by the author, and his diary is a work of fiction.

Library of Congress Cataloging-in-Publication Data
Hermes, Patricia.
A perfect place: Joshua's Oregon Trail diary / by Patricia Hermes.
p. cm. — (My America)

Summary: Late in 1848, nine-year-old Joshua McCullough starts a second journal, this time recording events in Willamette Valley, Oregon Territory, as his family and others they met on the trail begin to get settled.

ISBN 0-439-19999-9; 0-439-38900-3 (pbk.)

[1. Frontier and pioneer life — Oregon — Fiction. 2. Family life — Oregon — Fiction. 3. Oregon — History — To 1859 — Fiction. 4. Diaries — Fiction.] I. Title. II. Series.
PZ7.H4317 Pe 2002

[Fic] — dc21   2002019078
CIP AC

10 9 8 7 6 5   06

The display type was set in Cooper Old Style.
The text type was set in Goudy.
Book design by Elizabeth B. Parisi
Photo research by Dwayne Howard

Printed in the U.S.A. 23
First edition, November 2002